# BOATS

by Anne Rockwell

PUFFIN BOOKS

PUFFIN BOOKS
Published by the Penguin Group
Penguin Putnam Books for Young Readers,
345 Hudson Street, New York, New York 10014, U.S.A.
Penguin Books Ltd, 27 Wrights Lane, London W8 5TZ, England
Penguin Books Australia Ltd, Ringwood, Victoria, Australia
Penguin Books Canada Ltd, 10 Alcorn Avenue, Toronto, Ontario, Canada M4V 3B2
Penguin Books (N.Z.) Ltd, 182-190 Wairau Road, Auckland 10, New Zealand
Penguin Books Ltd, Registered Offices: Harmondsworth, Middlesex, England

Library of Congress number 82-2420
ISBN 978-0-14-054988-1

Published in the United States by Dutton Children's Books,
a division of Penguin Books USA Inc.
345 Hudson Street, New York, N.Y. 10014

Editor: Ann Durell   Designer: Isabel Warren-Lynch

Manufactured in China by South China Printing Co.
First Unicorn Edition 1985      COBE

28  30  29

Boats float.

They float on quiet ponds,

and busy rivers,

and the wide, blue sea.

Some boats are big.

Some boats are small.

Some boats go fast.

Some boats go slow.

What makes a boat go?
Oars and paddles make some boats go.

Wind-filled sails make others go.

Motors and engines make some boats go,

and barges are pulled or pushed by tugs.

There are boats for work

and boats for play.

On all the busy waters of our world,

there are boats.